Jimmy John the
By Ken Hinman

Illustrated by
Trish Gename

Dedications

Dedicated to my wife Carol for her love, friendship, dedication, and understanding of me for over fifty years.

A special thanks to Marvin Cutler for giving me the idea of writing this book.

To Susan Klotz, editor and project manager, who was determined to see this book in print.

To Trish Gename and her beautiful illustrations.

To Steve Hopkins III, Clay Ebert, and John Krag for all their help and advice when restoring this tractor.

Copyright © 2012, Kenneth Hinman

All rights reserved. No part of the material protected by this copyright notice may be reproduced in whole or in part in any form without the express written permission from the copyright owner. For permission to reproduce selections from this book, write to Kenneth Hinman, 705 Skipjack, Henderson, NV, 89015 ATTN: Permissions. Cover and original Illustrations by Trish Gename are also protected by this copyright.

ISBN -13: 978-0-615-71086-0
ISBN -10: 0615710867

Acknowledgements

This little book was published with the support of the following friends and family of Ken Hinman.
We took his wonderful story and ran with it!

Jenn, Mike, Justin & Breanna Adams

Amanda Burns

Captain Jack's Restaurant

Margery Cape

Randy Cape

Bill and Lisa Chandler

Karen Manely Duggan

Gary and Denise Freeburg

Russell and Beulah Freeburg

Todd and Jane Freeburg

Jon, Jeni Jo, Jack and Emma Foster

Jim Hanway

Ruth Hanway

Bonnie Harrington

Dan Hinman and Shelby Cass

Dana Hinman

Don and Helen Hinman

Ed and Marjoire Hinman

John Hinman

Katherine Jo Hinman

Mike Hinman

Mary Hinman

Wendell (Wendy) Hinman

Mardra Horse

Rusty and Nomi Johnson

Camey and Terry Robert Johnson

Mike Kennedy

Ann and Charles King

Lillie Lee

Renee Melody

Gil Marr

Retta O'Meara (Loretta Hinman)

Vikki Robb-Aquadro

Derrick, Gail, Amber, and Abby Robinson

Virginia Salisbury

Daniel and Cory Jo Schultz

Margaret St. John

Amy Taylor

Virgil and Gina Weese

Phil and Pat Williams

Once upon a time...

...in a place called Iowa,
in a big factory where people worked long hours
making tractors, a very special little tractor was made.

It was February 25th, 1944,
and that was a very long time ago.

This special little tractor was painted a beautiful
bright green and his wheels were painted
a very pretty yellow.

In fact, to this very day, they still paint
tractors the same green and yellow
at that factory in Iowa.

When the tractor was all assembled, he looked at himself.
Then looked at himself again.
He was flabbergasted!
He was such a beautiful tractor and he liked what he saw!

The factory workers knew at once that this was a very special tractor, for when they started it, the tractor went ...

Jimmy John, Jimmy John, Jimmy John

The workers were very alarmed. They tried and tried to find out why the tractor made this very unusual sound. They worked and worked on it, but to no avail. Each time they started the tractor, it did the same thing!

Jimmy John, Jimmy John, Jimmy John

Finally they just decided there was nothing they could do with him and they would just have to let him go through life making this unusual but happy sound.
So it was that the workers named the tractor Jimmy John.

The very next day, Jimmy John and a big tractor were loaded on a truck and off they went to Sidney, Nebraska. When they arrived, some friendly men unloaded both tractors and put them in a big building.

A few days later, a man came in, started the big tractor up, and drove it out. Jimmy John was so sad that his friend was gone. He just sat there all alone in the dark.

Then one day, the big doors opened and Jimmy John could see a rather short, slim man walking toward him. The man was tanned from the sun and had a wrinkled pleasant face. "Hello, I'm Farmer Vern." Jimmy John had never heard such a kind voice.

Farmer Vern walked all around Jimmy John. Then he climbed up and sat on the seat. He put his hands on Jimmy John's steering wheel and said in his soft pleasant voice, "You will do. You will do just fine."

Farmer Vern drove Jimmy John out into the bright sunlight, loaded him on his truck, and away they went! Up out of the valley and across the rolling hills they drove. Jimmy John could see fields and fields of green wheat waving in the gentle breeze.

They drove through a quiet little town
and everyone waved at them.

Then they turned up a dirt road, climbed a long hill, crossed some railroad tracks and finally pulled up to a farmhouse sitting among some trees. "This must be my home!" Jimmy John thought.

Farmer Vern unloaded him from the truck and drove him into a big barn, just as the sun was setting. What a glorious, brilliant, red sunset it was!

Farmer Vern closed the doors, and knowing this was to be his home, Jimmy John fell fast asleep. He was very happy.

The very next morning when it was just light enough to see,
Jimmy John was awakened by a little boy
peeking inside the door at him.

The boy was wearing bib overalls and a red shirt. He had curly red
hair and freckles. "Hi, I'm Ken," said the little boy.

Ken walked around Jimmy John and looked at him from his front to his back, and from his tall exhaust to the bottom of his tires. Then he climbed up and sat on the seat, put his hands on the steering wheel and whispered, "I like you."

Just then Farmer Vern came through the big doors. "May I drive the tractor?" asked Ken. Farmer Vern smiled. "Ken you are just too small, but soon you will grow bigger and stronger and then you can help with the farm work and drive Jimmy John."

Year after year, Farmer Vern and Jimmy John worked on the farm. They plowed the soil, and planted and harvested crops of wheat, corn, oats, and barley. They mowed and baled hay.

Ken watched and learned and waited for the day when he would be big enough to drive Jimmy John and help with the farming.

Then one spring, Farmer Vern and Ken went to the barn.
Jimmy John could not believe what he saw.
Ken had grown into a strong young man!

Farmer Vern said,
"Ken, start up Jimmy John and go hook up the plow."
Jimmy John was so happy, he nearly bounced right up
off the ground!

They worked all summer. They plowed the soil and planted and harvested the crops. They mowed and baled the hay. They worked many springs and summers. They had a grand time and became very good friends.

Then one spring day, Farmer Vern came to get Jimmy John ready for plowing but Ken was not there.

All spring and summer, Jimmy John and Farmer Vern did all the things that needed doing on the farm, but Jimmy John wondered where Ken was.

One afternoon just as the sun was about to go down, Jimmy John saw someone standing by the farmhouse. At first he could not see who it was, then suddenly he realized it was Ken, standing there wearing an Army uniform with a big smile on his face.

For the next few days, Ken and Jimmy John went to the field and baled hay, just as they had always done.
Oh, they had such a good time!

Then Ken told Jimmy John that he must go and complete his Army training, but that he would be back one day.

The seasons passed, and Jimmy John and Farmer Vern continued farming, growing older each year.

Farmer Vern found it harder and harder to climb up and sit on Jimmy John's seat. Jimmy John found it harder and harder to pull the plow and do all the things he had once done so easily.

One day as they were working, Farmer Vern stopped to rest. He was very, very tired. In his soft gentle voice, he told Jimmy John that he was going to have to quit farming because they were both getting too old to do the hard work.

Jimmy John knew he was right.

In a few days, a man came and loaded Jimmy John onto his truck. Farmer Vern came out to wave goodbye and looked very sad.

They drove across the valley, and stopped at a farm. Jimmy John was unloaded and parked by a fence where he sat all alone. He was very sad. He couldn't understand why they didn't let him work anymore. Was it because he was old?

Jimmy John just sat there in the field by the fence, year after year.

His muffler became rusty and fell off, his tires lost their air and went flat. His bright yellow wheels faded.

Then one cold and dreary November day, Jimmy John saw someone walking toward him. He couldn't tell who it was because he couldn't see very well anymore. Oh well, it didn't matter anyway because no one ever came to see him.

So he simply looked away and sighed.
But the person walked right up to him!

Then he walked all around him.

"Hello old friend," said the man, with tears of joy running down his cheeks. "I have been looking for you for a long time and I'm so glad I finally found you!"

Jimmy John thought he recognized his voice. "Is this someone I should know?" he thought.

The man stepped closer and laid a warm hand on Jimmy John's cold hood.

It was Ken!

Jimmy John was so glad to see Ken again that he began to cry happy tears. It was a grand reunion!

Ken loaded Jimmy John onto a trailer and took him home to Mississippi where it wasn't quite so cold.
Ken unloaded him into the green, grassy yard.

The very next morning, Ken started taking Jimmy John all apart until nearly all his parts were all over the yard!

What in the world? Was this any way to treat an old friend?

Ken carefully cleaned and painted all of Jimmy John's parts the very exact color of green and yellow that he was when he was a brand new tractor.
Then Ken reassembled Jimmy John's parts one by one, putting them all back just where they belonged.

Jimmy John was very happy. He wanted to jump up and shake and laugh just as he had done all those years ago, but he was just too old. He simply looked at Ken and gave him a great big smile.

Ken was very pleased.

They both felt young again!

On the very day that Ken finished getting Jimmy John all cleaned up and reassembled, there was to be a parade in town.

Ken started Jimmy John's motor and climbed up on his seat.

The tractor went **Jimmy John, Jimmy John, Jimmy John, Jimmy John,** and away they went to the parade!

All the mothers and fathers and children cheered, clapped their hands and waved.

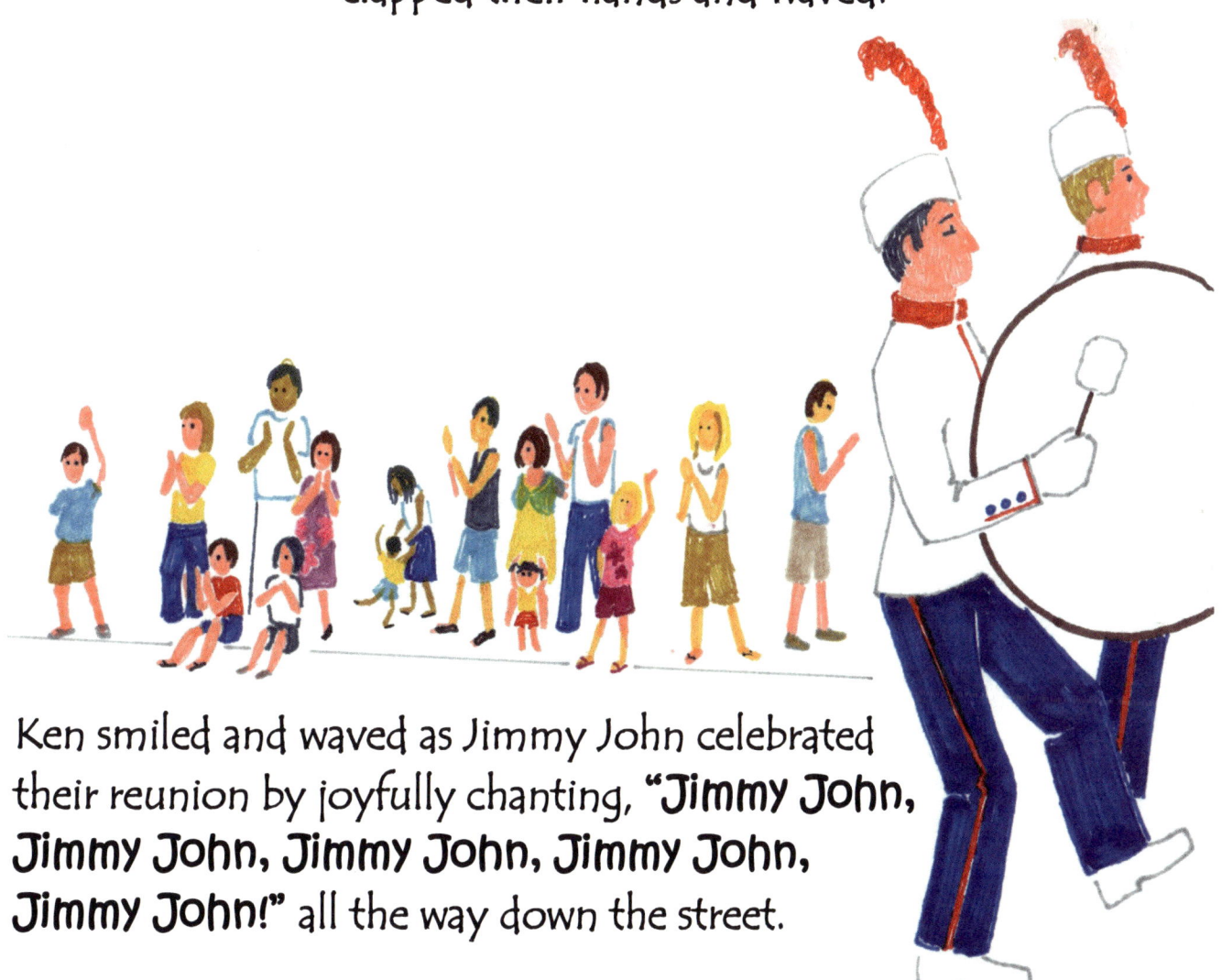

Ken smiled and waved as Jimmy John celebrated their reunion by joyfully chanting, **"Jimmy John, Jimmy John, Jimmy John, Jimmy John, Jimmy John!"** all the way down the street.

Ken and Jimmy John were very, very happy to be together again!

CPSIA information can be obtained
at www.ICGtesting.com
Printed in the USA
BVIC01n2120140813
328642BV00001B